CHARLES FUGE AND DAVID CONWAY

Bedtime Hullabaloo!

Hodder
Children's
Books

A division of Hachette Children's Books

ONE NIGHT IN THE SILLY SAVANNAH
a ludicrous leopard was leapfrogging to bed when
all of a sudden there was a terrible racket...

'What a hullabaloo!' said the leopard and decided to follow the noise.

Along the way the leopard
passed by a dozy giraffe
singing a lullaby when all
of a sudden...

HHHRRR-ZZZ!

SNORT, SNORT!

Bedtime Hullabaloo!

'FOR ALL THE STAFF AT ST PETER IN CHAINS
RC INFANT SCHOOL' D.C.

Bedtime Hullabaloo!

Written by David Conway

The right of David Conway to be identified as the author and
Charles Fuge as the illustrator of this Work has been asserted
by them in accordance with the Copyright, Designs
and Patents Act 1988.

ISBN: 978 0 340 98126 9
10 9 8 7 6 5 4 3 2 1

Printed in China

Hodder Children's Books is a division
of Hachette Children's Books.
An Hachette UK Company.

www.hachette.co.uk

MIX
Paper from
responsible sources
FSC® C010256
FSC
www.fsc.org

Goodnight Moon © 1947 by Harper & Row.
Text renewed 1975 by Roberta Brown Rauch.
Illustrations © renewed by Edith Hurd, Clement Hurd,
John Thacher Hurd and George Hellyer,
as Trustees of the Edith & Clement Hurd 1982 Trust.
Used by permission of HarperCollins Publishers.

'What a hullabaloo!' said the giraffe and decided to follow the noise.

The leopard and
the giraffe then met a
baboon who was reading
a bedtime story to the moon
when all of a sudden...

HHHRRR-ZZZ!

SNORT, SNORT!
GRUNT, GRUNT!

'What a hullabaloo!' said the baboon and decided to follow the noise.

The three animals followed the noise
to check out all the fuss and discover
the source of this bedtime din, this
clamour, this hubbub, this rumpus.

Under the still starlit night they walked.
The noise began to swell.

More and more animals joined in the search
to seek out the nuisance as well. There was
a hat-wearing hyena half asleep, a music-making
meerkat counting sheep...

...a zany zebra who was having a dream about sailing upon a sea of ice cream,

a sleepwalking lion with bedraggled hair,
an outraged ostrich clutching a teddy bear,
and a polka-dot, pyjama-wearing water buffalo.

So on they all walked into the night, all sleepy
and tired and very uptight. Through the long

and when at last they came to a stop what on
earth did they see?

But a tiny shrew, wearing a pink tutu, snoring her head off very loudly.

HHHRRR-ZZZ!

SNORT, SNORT! GRUNT, GRUNT!

Something had to be done. Leopard growled as loud as he could. Giraffe bleated even louder.

Baboon screeched with
all his might until...

...the terrible racket woke the shrew from her thunderous slumber.

And all was quiet on the Silly Savannah,
so quiet you couldn't hear a peep...

BUT NOT FOR LONG!